Box Girls

"The chorus of voices in Aria Braswell's stunning *Box Girls* is by turns mesmerizing, heartbreaking, and creepy as hell. In telling the collective story of a group of female performers, the novel asks what it means to be an observer and what it means to be perceived as an object. *Box Girls* is a demanding and grippingly intelligent exploration of power, isolation, and control, and Braswell herself is an unmissable new talent."

— Lauren Grodstein, author of the *New York Times* bestseller *A Friend of the Family*

Box Girls
Aria Braswell

LIMIT ZERO Publications
Portland, Oregon

This book is published by LIMIT ZERO Publications
www.LMTzero.com

Cover Design by Joel Amat Güell
joelamatguell.com

Interior Design by Gigi Little
gigilittle.com

Published in the United States of America
ISBN 978-1-938753-50-3

The Strasbourg, and the contents of her belly,
now sit, a decomposing thing.

Years before, the hotel stood, a proud beacon on
Hollywood Boulevard, hailed for its Box Girls—
an enigmatic art installation featuring women
suspended in themed glass displays—until abruptly
shutting its doors and boarding its windows in 2007.

What follows is the transcription of a record log,
taken on site, cataloging witness statements from
the Box Girls as they recount the death of a
co-worker that occurred on shift.

001 [interview labeled] 06.21 eve
002 [interview labeled] 06.21 the poet
003 [interview labeled] 06.21 graffiti
008 [interview labeled] 06.21 disco girl
010 [interview labeled] 06.21 the one on the bed
013 [interview labeled] 06.21 apocalypse
015 [interview labeled] 06.21 eve
017 [interview labeled] 06.21 paper snowflakes
018 [interview labeled] 06.22 the naked one
020 [interview labeled] 06.22 graffiti
023 [interview labeled] 06.22 paper snowflakes
024 [interview labeled] 06.22 cosmonaut
026 [interview labeled] 06.23 the coffin
028 [interview labeled] 06.23 disco girl
030 [interview labeled] 06.23 paper snowflakes
032 [interview labeled] 06.23 the poet
034 [interview labeled] 06.23 the one on the bed
036 [interview labeled] 06.23 graffiti
037 [interview labeled] 06.24 cosmonaut
039 [interview labeled] 06.24 the poet
042 [interview labeled] 06.24 the one on the bed
043 [interview labeled] 06.24 disco girl
048 [interview labeled] 06.24 eve
049 [interview labeled] 06.24 the naked one
051 [interview labeled] 06.25 the one on the bed
052 [interview labeled] 06.25 paper snowflakes

211 [interview labeled] 07.30 paper snowflakes
212 [interview labeled] 07.30 the naked one

213 [interview labeled] 08.03 the coffin

214 [interview labeled] 08.05 graffiti

217 [interview labeled] 08.10 disco girl

220 [interview labeled] 08.22 paper snowflakes

221 [interview labeled] 09.01 Michael, The Archangel

06.21
eve

I'm sorry.

It's making me very nervous.

Sorry for apologizing to you. Unless you'd like me to.
Apologize for something. I'm sorry. I'm not sure what
this is. I've been told I have a guilty conscience.

Can I come back in a moment?

06.21
the poet

If you want me to start, I'll start, but I think it's only fair to warn them. I can go do it, if you'd like, and you can wait here. I don't think any of the other girls know what this is. I'll go tell them what to do and you can wait. I only need to know what to say.

I need to know what to say.

Or I could guess.

Alright, I'll guess. Just the answers, then, without the questions?

I'll go tell them.

06.21
graffiti

It feels funny is all. Talking with you. Well, *at* you.
None of us do much of that here. Much talking. It's a
sort of unspoken part of the job description.

I didn't mean to make a joke there, but I have a
habit of doing that. I don't think I'm very funny, but
everyone is always laughing at me and I think it's
because I say things wrong sometimes? I never say
things wrong around the girls, though, because, as
I said, we don't do much talking, so there's not as
much opportunity.

Some of us share a cigarette in the parking lot now
and again, but what's there to talk about, really?
That's just the nature of the job. It's individualistic or
isolating, and—I almost said idiosyncratic. Isn't that
funny? It's because I'm nervous.

Usually, you make friends with girls from work when

you're working regular sorts of jobs, because you have them for company all day, folding blue jeans and what not. But not here. You really only have yourself for company here. That doesn't mean I don't wonder about the other girls. I do. That's basically what I do all night. And that's exactly why we can't do much talking.

I've already got these ideas of what each of them are like inside my head. Sometimes, their personalities suit the rooms they're in. Sometimes, they don't. Like the one who's painting her toes. In my head, she's a really great actress, because she never paints her toes outside of work. She'd never paint her toes in real life. But she does it here and looks real natural doing it, because, in my head, she's a really great actress. I don't know if that's true. It's just one of those truths I've given her. If I actually got to know her and found out she does, in fact, paint her toes outside the box, it might confuse me or give me an aneurism, because I won't know who I'm looking at or talking to. I'm not sure if aneurysms work that way. I imagine one could be caused by something like that. Or it might feel like experiencing a loss. I'd have to mourn the version of her I'd come up with.

I wonder if they wonder about me? The other girls. If they see me in my box and think I'm rather street smart?

The one I like best wears the space suit. I've never seen her face, but I feel I know her better than any of the other girls. In my head, she's chewing gum inside that helmet constantly, blowing big pink bubbles and popping them with her teeth just before they hit the visor. It's her secret, again, in my head, because chewing gum could be a breach of her contract. I don't really know what's in her contract, because I've only read mine, but maybe it says that in hers? *No gum*. But she chews it anyway. Always chewing and chewing. And she comes into work with it hidden beneath her tongue, and pulls the helmet on before anyone can be the wiser? And she blows bubbles for eight hours straight because she loves the feeling it gives her. The risk.

I'm envious of her. I wish I was that kind of brave. I'm not great with small spaces, even though I sit all night inside a box, so, that's something.

But it's not her you want to talk about. And I doubt you want to talk more about the one who paints her toes? You don't, do you?

You're here about the other one? That one's a sadder story, less fun to think about.

I think she was eating them. The bees.

Didn't they find a bunch of bees inside her?

06.21
disco girl

I didn't see any blood. I'll admit to looking for it, though. Is being curious a crime? We're in the middle of one, aren't we? Isn't that why you're here? Besides, there's no tape up. No yellow or red, the dangerous colors. And besides, I was off the clock. I made a point of getting here earlier than usual today so I could check to see if things were different.

I get to places early. It's important to be in control of your space in order to perform to your best abilities. I don't remember where I learned that. Maybe I came up with it myself? Either way, I wanted to see if there was any remnant of anything left inside her box that might contribute to things being different now.

But I didn't see any blood. I didn't see any cracks in the glass, or papier-mâché bees on the floor or missing from their wires, or even a change in the lighting. Everything here is exactly the same as it always has been, except that we've crossed into some alternate dimension where we can flicker out inside our boxes without a single sound.

06.21
the one on the bed

I get this feeling that comes over me. Like, the place
is bugged. Like, I'm the bug. I guess that's what it
means to be a fly on the wall. But, God, it makes
me feel good about myself. Like, I'm serving some
greater governmental purpose, because that's what
I'm really doing in there is listening. I guess that's
why you want to speak with me?

I'm jealous of your jobs, actually. I think I'd be good
at investigation. It'd make me feel sexier. I know that.
I'd walk into a bar after a long shift of investigation,
just oozing sex. Because that's what sex is, isn't
it? Having a secret? The secretness of sex? People
always think my job is sexy. But it's boring. I'm just a
woman in a box.

I don't think they know we can hear them.

I listen all night to people embarrassing themselves.

People really are so embarrassing when they think you can't hear them. Mostly, they ask the front desk if I get to use the bathroom. I think they assume the glass is soundproof, but it isn't. I'd go crazy in there if it was. Seven whole hours of *me*? I couldn't take that. Most of the time, when I'm holding the book, I'm not really reading. I'm just scanning the words on the page and listening. I get embarrassed so easily for other people. What is that?

I'm lucky mine even has books. Nail polish for my toes. I assume the box with the spray-painted walls smells awful and I'd rather be stuck smelling paper and glue. Ironically, I'm not much of a reader. But the words on the page are a nice something to pretend to look at while I sit and pretend I'm not listening.

As long as I'm in here, I don't exist in real life in the real world. I don't even feel my body anymore, aside from my ears, when I go in.

I wish they'd take the pillows out though. They look too much like the ones in the rooms upstairs and I think some people take that as a suggestion. I've had a man ask the desk how much I cost. I heard him. If that's not embarrassing, I don't know what is. But it was the first time in here I felt I wasn't all ears.

06.21
apocalypse

I didn't know until they told me. I don't face her.

I think I was actually the last of us to know what'd
happened. I've seen her box before, but not *her* in it.
There was a different girl in there before her, who
had the box when I first started working nights here,
and she always seemed tired.

It's not a good box. Maybe that was the issue. All
those little bees on wires. Too crowded. She could
hardly itch her face in there without bumping one
with the back of her hand. Maybe that was the issue.
It's always dim in there, like a sunset. Maybe that's
the issue. It's weird to spend time in light that exists
in a half state. It can be disorienting. Could you
imagine if dusk lasted any longer than it does? What
it'd do to our brains?

Mine isn't a good box, either. No one likes seeing

Lady Liberty lying in the dirt like that.

I'm not saying she did it to herself, on purpose, or anything. Like I said, I don't face her. But you never know people's brains. Maybe that was the issue.

06.21
eve

I was a bit nervous earlier, because I'd never met you, but it's fine now.

I'd still rather not talk about her, if that's okay? I don't like dwelling on the bad. I've found it's best to not question why certain things happen and just be thankful it didn't happen to you.

I like the themes. I think it's fun and I don't mind mine being such an obvious one. At first, I was exhausted by the concept of it. One apple to fill seven hours with? But, after a while, it's become such a meditative thing that I look forward to it all day. I wake up thinking about it. *An apple a day*. That's something they say, you know, and it's reassuring.

The best part is, I've never had to time out all the chewing. There were times, in the beginning, when I got down to the core too fast and had to spend the rest of the night picking around the seeds with my teeth. But my jaw figured things out, once it got used to how a night felt inside the box, and it configured just how long I needed to chew, the size of bites to take to survive it, and how to never want more than I was given.

I'm a better person now because of it. A happier person. See, this box was designed for me. I was very lucky. I'm very thankful.

I wasn't a religious person, before the box. But I understand it now, having a practice. A ritual ties you to something. But mine isn't a connection to some higher power. Mine is the feel of the peel on my lips before my very first bite, and knowing that I am, for seven hours straight, fulfilling a need that is human. And, because of that, I never doubt that I am one.

06.21
paper snowflakes

Did they ever cut her open to see what was inside? I can't really talk today, I've decided. Thank you. But, don't I know you from somewhere?

06.22
the naked one

I'm not sure how much you want to know about me
outside of it. I'm an artist and that's all. This is the
way I afford it.

I saw the ad and right away knew I'd have the job, if
I wanted it. Because I'm not shy about bodies, and
I know what looks good to a male and female gaze.
How to pose to suit the both of them.

I paint female figures a lot. I have one and know what
I'd like mine to look like. I know what's attractive
to the eye. If I were the one who made the boxes,
though, I'd have us sitting inside them as ugly as
possible, because it's a much more interesting thing
to look at. People grow tired of beautiful things. They
don't realize how uncompelling it all is, but you see
people's real tastes if you start to look at each other.
We seek out grotesque things all the time. We slow
down to look at traffic accidents. We get sucked

down one-a.m. rabbit holes reading about the Night Stalker or the Golden State Killer or whoever else is slaughtering a bay area somewhere. We pop pimples in the mirror because we like seeing pus break through skin.

But, the ones who made the boxes want beautiful things inside them, so, that's how I am. I don't suspect The Managers are artists. That much is clear.

I'd argue, if I were lying in my box and the woman in the box across from mine was peeling the skin off her feet, you'd rather watch her, wouldn't you? If they'd left that girl's corpse in her box, I can assure you, not one person, all night, would look at me in mine.

06.22
graffiti

I saw her talking, not too long ago, to the one in the
go-go boots, upset about something. I'd never seen
them talking before. Like I said, we don't do much
talking. She had her hands up over her ears and her
face was all red and she was taking these big deep
breaths. I almost bumped her with the service door
on my way to the lot. It surprised me.

I've noticed the girls try and time their journeys at
the end of a shift, another thing we all do but don't
talk about, so we don't bump into each other on our
way out the door. It's better that way, I think, to time
our footsteps, down from the boxes once the lights
go out, to our lockers, through the service corridor,
and out to the back lot, that way we avoid any
awkward chatter. There's no point in saying, "Have a
nice night," because the night is nearly over when we
all crawl out anyways. So, I was surprised the two of
them were standing out back together, is all I'm

saying. I don't have to talk so much, just tell me.

The back lot is dark. That part feels purposeful, like
it's kept that way to disillusion us from lingering
there. *Dissuade*, I mean. But still, I saw them, and it
felt sort of inappropriate to watch, like I was looking
at something I shouldn't, like I was breaching my
contract, even though we were done for the night.
Still, I looked away, and I got in my car, and when
the headlights came on, there she was again, leaning
against the building with her face all red.

And I remember thinking she sort of looked like a
little gray ghost, the way the streetlamp was on her.
Wispy and dim and afraid of something. I think if I'd
seen her walking along the road on my way home
that night, that's what I would've thought, that I
was seeing a ghost. It scares me that I ever had that
thought at all, now that she is one. Sometimes, when

I get in my car at the end of a shift and turn my headlights on, I see her, leaning against the building. Her face red, eyes wide, wispy, dim, afraid.

06.22
paper snowflakes

I wish you'd tell me what you found. I always felt
a tenderness for her. I don't know if it was love. I
wonder how it could be love? The only reason I think
it is, is because I'm hurting now.

Didn't they find a bunch of bees inside her?

I'm too tired to talk.

06.22
cosmonaut

I don't know how much I'm like them, if I am really much at all. That doesn't make me special, does it? Even then? There's always someone like you somewhere, isn't there? That's what I worry, anyways.

I worry there's someone like me, who never left home, and that I'm mocking her when I put on the suit. Sometimes, art can be violence too, you know? Бьёт - значит любит.

But I didn't come here to be any one thing. Some of the other girls here seem to think the boxes they're in *mean* something. Like it's an extension of what they are.

But I'm just breath inside a helmet, a prop on a backdrop of stars. Maybe that is an extension of what I am, but I'd be better off in delusion, thinking I was the sun.

Maybe we all think that. Maybe one of us is right. Who am I to question if anyone here has planets revolving around them? Regardless, I'm not sure I believe the universe is expanding. I feel it, sometimes, closing in. But, then again, something is wrong with my box.

06.23
the coffin

I thought they were going to change mine. It feels like it would rub people the wrong way.

It's making me feel sort of funny. I've begun to think I'm supposed to be playing *her*, when I'm in there. I can't help but do it, even if I tell myself not to. I feel myself sitting the way she used to, inside her box. Delicate, shuddering little thing. One leg over the other, chin resting on my knee. Sometimes I swat at a bee. Sometimes I eat one, just to test if it will kill me. I think I'm starting to look like her. You can just make out your own outline in the glass sometimes if the light's hitting it right, and I'm not entirely sure I remember what she used to look like but I'm starting to think it's similar to me.

No matter what, I feel like I shouldn't lie down.

This box didn't exist before I got here. They made it

for me. Some of our boxes are built like that; made for us specifically. But her box wasn't. It was built for the one before her. She never quite fit inside it the way the other one did. The light, deep golden light, like honey, didn't suit her features as well as it did the other girl. She didn't look ugly in there, just not right.

She felt it. She knew she was wrong for her box. I only know that because I can feel it now too, when I'm playing her, all that *wrongness* closing in around me, making me hungry for stingers. If I close my eyes, I feel the light isn't well suited for my features and know I've slipped into being her again. I'm starting to worry about how easy it's becoming.

But mostly I worry about them changing my box. Odds are, they'd have to change the girl inside it too, so I'm alright with being her, for now, if that's what they're asking.

06.23
disco girl

I'll see the same people come in sometimes. Please
don't tell my managers that.

I've never met them, you know. The Managers. I just
get their emails.

We're not supposed to look at the guests. It's in the
rule book not to look at them, because The Managers
don't want us breaking the "wall between worlds" or
something like that. It's written in the contract. But I
look. Please don't tell them that. Every now and then.
I don't know if it's to see if someone's watching me,
or to see the other girls. I think it helps to see the
girls sometimes because this whole thing feels more
like an ensemble that way, and less like I'm doing
something I shouldn't.

I can't look at the naked one, though. It makes me
afraid for the rest of us.

But sure, so, I look. Only when I need to. And I'll see the same people come in every now and then, the same people, and I keep going back to that night and all the nights before that one, trying to picture some familiarity in the ones that may have lingered at her box just a bit longer than they should have? We get men sometimes, most times it's men, who leer in longer than they should. Maybe she had one? Maybe that's what happened? Now and then, a girl will have one. It's a common symptom of the job. There are certain ones you have to worry about. Certain men will follow girls to their cars. I think that happened once a few months ago to the one who writes the poems. And then she stopped writing for a while. For a while, after that, she'd just sit.

06.23
paper snowflakes

I fall in love sort of easily. That's what I was on about last time, wasn't it? *Love*. I was thinking about last time, that's why it's on my mind.

Are you with the police? That's what this is, isn't it? Is that why you seem so familiar?

I'll keep on going, regardless, because I don't mind talking to you. I'll say, for your record, that I love people most from far away. It's not their looks. It's the not knowing much about them, I think. Sometimes, I wish my eyes weren't so good and that I was hard of hearing? Just because that would soften things up for me? It's easier to love something when it's soft.

She was soft from far away. And the light in her box was warm, so it made me think she was kind. And sweet, like honey is sweet.

I'm sure everyone who saw her from far off loved her too. We're all easier to love from far away, I think. Up close, we all look rather stuck.

Wow, does my heart really hurt.

06.23
the poet

Some kind of metaphor, huh? It's a disappointingly obvious one. Walled in on all sides, glass ceiling over our heads, but stuck inside for hours at a time seeing everything, feeling everything, alive by being looked at. Girls in boxes. I rolled my eyes the first time I came in here, thinking The Managers were getting at some kind of obvious metaphor. Just the one you're thinking. The one we're all thinking, if we've got even an iota of wrinkle in our brains.

Seems obvious, at first. But that's not what we're doing here. That's not the metaphor we're making. I know that now. I started becoming wise to it a few days in. Nobody realizes what it is we're really doing here. The real statement we're making here is lost on people.

All night, and nobody knew. Do you know how long she'd been—I know it's morbid to think about, but

I think all of us are curious how long we were—we want to know how long we were in a room with a dead thing.

Looking at a dead thing.

Our eyes brush past each other's boxes all the time. Just scanning the tops of the heads in the lobby. I wonder how many times I looked at her without knowing. I know that's morbid to think about—but I wonder how many people came in that night and saw her and didn't know. I wonder if anyone did know and kept it to themselves, or how it felt to be the one that finally realized she was—as cold as she was—and had to do something about it.

I wonder what it feels like to realize what you're *really* looking at.

06.23
the one on the bed

I'd say we were friends. I'd say that just to say it,
but it isn't quite true. By *friends*, I really mean we
shared a cigarette once or twice after a shift, and
that's the most time I've spent with one of the girls
outside of work.

She didn't know what she was doing here. Just
stumbled into it, I think. A dancer, I think, maybe
ballet? Ballet dancers smoke cigarettes. And she had
small bones.

She didn't really like her box. She mentioned that it
didn't suit her. She asked me what sound played in
mine and I told her there wasn't any. I didn't know
any of the boxes had their own sounds. The one
before her hadn't mentioned one and I wonder when
they made that change. She told me she could hear
a buzzing inside of hers, which makes sense, consid-
ering the bees. But I told her maybe it was just

electricity running into a bulb. She told me it made
her want to rip her ears off. She told me she was
losing her hair.

I thought I knew so much about her, compared to the
others, but that didn't sound like much, did it?

What happened to the one before her? I shared
a cigarette with her once too, and now I don't
remember the color of her hair.

06.23
graffiti

Isn't it funny that she was allergic to bees? Not
funny, no, I'll think of the word.

Maybe it's just a rumor. I'm realizing now I never
fact-checked that, but maybe I read it in an article
somewhere? Or maybe I heard it from one of the girls
on the way to my car?

Ironic, is what I meant earlier. I don't think it's funny.
I want that on record, please.

06.24
cosmonaut

Something is wrong with my box.

I've known something was wrong. Last week, I said
something to someone about my box feeling smaller.
Was that you? I almost emailed management. But I
was afraid of people making jokes. I didn't want them
to say it was me getting bigger. 'Cause that'd be a
breach of contract.

I know my box. I know how many seconds it takes to
slide my toes along the glass floor to each edge of it,
so I know the walls are an inch further *in* now than
before. It's just enough further in that no one else
would notice the difference, aside from me. I can't
be in there anymore without feeling my heart in my
chest the whole time, like its box has gotten smaller
too so it has no space to beat without hitting my ribs.

But I haven't gotten bigger. That'd be a breach of

contract.

If this is going to be confidential, I want to tell you something else too. The stars in the backdrop. They're these little LEDs, hundreds of them, maybe. Well, there used to be hundreds. But I started noticing every time I had my back turned, it'd get a little bit darker in there. A little bit darker each time. There are less stars than there were before. Tiny bulbs going out. So, I started staring. As long as I stare at them, they stay on. But every time I look away, I can feel the darkness, like a sheet across my back.

And I know that something is wrong. I know it's a sort of game. I know, one day, if I'm not careful, I'll look away at the wrong time and the stars will all go out.

06.24
the poet

There was a man once who'd grown interested in me
because of something I'd written him. It's not in my
contract that I can't look at the guests. I'm an exception to the rule. So, I do look, because that's the func-
tion of my box. It was me who'd pitched the idea to
management, when I first heard about the exhibition.
And I knew when I pitched it, that it'd be a dangerous
job. I meant it to be temporary, and it will be. A
featured installation. I wanted to share my art and
sell my work. You can look me up. You can find me. I
want to be found. I'm the only one here who's not an
anonymous part of some display. I'm the artist, not
the art, and I knew that meant facing a threat. A lot
goes on between eyes. As soon as you look someone
in theirs, you create a bridge. You always feel it.
It's insurmountable. It's a very easy way to write a
poem. And the eyes are all I get. Sometimes, they'll
say things to me, through the glass, but I won't allow
myself to listen. I try to make it as authentic, as spur

of the moment as possible, whatever comes to me the second I create that bridge.

Do I remember what I wrote him? Of course not. I hold no sentimentality for anything I write and forget as soon as it comes out of me. You can't tell if I'm being sarcastic. I can tell by your eyes, by our bridge, but I can't become sentimental about a string of words I'll never see again the moment they leave my box through a mail slot. So, no. I can't tell you if he was angry or turned on, but knowing the person who followed me out to my car was a man, and knowing what men do to women alone in the dark, I would reckon it was one of the two, or both.

It probably went something like:

So so distinctly green are those two things.

Call it envy of a god, handing out psalms to be consumed like the breath of life,

Or the infantile modernity of the very first one ever taken.

Perhaps he was confused. I'm a writer, not a fortune teller.

06.24
the one on the bed

I think the bed is harder.

That's all I have to say today.

06.24
disco girl

I didn't bring this up before, because it didn't feel important. She was just a nervous person, I think. Not very rational, a little flighty. I only ever had the one interaction with her, so that's the only basis I have for any of this, but it's how I'd started to think of her. I didn't bring it up before because it felt like it might be disrespectful. And I respect the dead. But I know someone's told you about a conversation they weren't a part of and, so, in order to not contribute to rumors, I'll share with you what happened. But don't tell my managers.

My box is next to hers, off to the side, so she always sits, sat, somewhere inside my periphery. One night, there was a lot of movement to my left, so I looked. Breach of contract, I know, but it was an odd amount of movement, and I couldn't help it. And, when I did, she turned and she looked directly at me, right in my eyes, and just held them there. I got scared someone would see, so I looked away. But I knew the look.

She was asking for help. I thought she'd gotten her period or something. I couldn't do anything to help with that, so I kept my eyes to myself, but for the rest of our shift I could feel hers still, boring into my cheek. It burned. I knew she was asking for something. But I couldn't help her. Not until we were out of our boxes, anyway. And when we were, out of our boxes, she just stayed staring. I could feel it on my way out the door and I stopped and I asked her what she was doing.

When I finally let myself look at her eyes again, they were all red and swollen and wider than I've ever seen. She scared me, to look at her. And I asked her again what she was doing and she told me she could still hear it. That she could hear it when she was driving home and lying in bed and that it followed her to work and got louder every time she sat inside her box. And I asked her what she was talking about and what she was hearing, but she just shoved her hands over her ears and told me she could hear it coming from my mouth and from everybody's mouths whenever anyone spoke to her and that she'd thought about stabbing herself in the ears but knew even then she'd still be able to hear it. Because it followed her. And she asked me to press my ear to her chest, begged me to see if I could hear it too. Coming from inside of her. Of course, I didn't check. I wouldn't have known what I was listening for.

I wanted to go home.

I didn't know if she'd always been like that, or if she

was having a panic attack, or if she was on some sort of new medication.

My sister has panic attacks and they sort of turn her inside out. And she takes pills, so—

I tried to ask her if she needed a glass of water, but as soon as I opened my mouth she started this terrible sobbing, drowning me out, getting redder and redder and her eyes wider, her hands pressing into her ears so hard I thought she'd crush her skull.

I could hardly look at her like that, all lit up in the headlights of someone's car. Like she was the top of a lit match. Burning. Burning. So bright it hurt my eyes. So bright it hurt to see.

So, I went home.

I didn't bring it up before because she never told me that night what she was so afraid of. I think some times about what I might have heard if I'd held my ear up to her chest, and wonder if it was contagious.

06.24
eve

I guess I—

Well, I guess my feelings are a bit hurt.

I've never had one that isn't sweet. In all my time here, the apple has always been sweet, never bitter. The thing is, well, I expect for it to be sweet. And this feels sort of careless, is all. I don't understand why I deserve carelessness, seeing how all I've ever done is exactly as I'm asked.

I wonder if you might ask where they get the apples from. I always thought they came from the hotel. That's a little silly of a thought to have, isn't it? Do I really think they grow them here? Inside the box they built for me?

I think that might be exactly what happens.

06.24
the naked one

I feel someone's eyes on me all the time.

That's to be expected, right? Because I'm all skin?
But *that* I'm used to. *This* is different. A girl feels a
look in her gut. It can feel like a punch, or a twist of
your organs, or butterflies. Bees?

Must be evolutionary, I don't know.

Some kind of internal mechanism built in to help
with decision making? Like, in determining how fast
a pace to walk, when to cross the street, or when to
hold your keys like a weapon? But *this* is different.
I don't even feel it in my gut. I feel it in my face.
Hanging on me like a heat, like someone is searing
themselves into me.

I think it's one of the girls,

I don't know how I know, but I do. It's one of the girls with her eyes on me. Has to be. Because it's the same feeling every night.

I can feel it but can't find it. I can't tell which one it is. I try not to look, because that would be a breach of contract. But if one of them is looking at me? That's a breach of contract on their end. Not that I'm a snitch, but—

I'll let myself look at the other boxes sometimes, if it's a slow night. I'll pretend I'm glancing up at the ceiling, pretending that I heard something. I never catch a pair of eyes glancing my way, but I can feel them. They burn.

06.25
the one on the bed

I want to know what you know.

We've heard nothing from The Managers since she was
pulled out. Have you spoken to them? Do you know
what they look like? Or how many of them there are?

I figure they've been here without us knowing, while
we're in the boxes, just making sure they made the
right choices with us. But we wouldn't know, with
the rules, anyhow, when they're here and when
they're not. And we wouldn't know which faces to
look for in any crowd if they were. None of us have
seen them. We don't know if they're men or women,
or what, or who.

Have they told you if we might be in danger?

Can I tell you how I heard they found her, and if it's
true?

06.25
paper snowflakes

I'm falling apart, really. I have a little sick feeling in my chest. I can be an emotional person but this version of me—I'm having trouble eating. Maybe my heart is broken, but, no, I think it's more than that. I think I might be dying.

I am. I'm dying.

I sit still as I can in the winter of the box they made for me, knowing what happens when I'm not careful enough, knowing how easy it is to do violence on delicate things. My wonderland's hung up by strings, white paper pieces that fall all the time. And they never put them back up, you know, when the pieces fall down, or get crinkled or torn, or ripped from the root when they're caught in the bend of my arm. Once a damage is done, they collect in a heap at my knees. I worry what happens when the last piece rips, falls, and I find myself sitting in spring.

I've always known it was coming, the ripping from the root, the dying part, but now I really feel it happening. I can feel my body stopping. I can feel the blood in my veins slowing down, my lungs taking in less and less air. I feel the skin on my face aging. Has that ever happened to you? Where you can feel it? It isn't a recent development. It started when I moved to the city. By the second day, I could feel the lines tunneling beneath the skin on my face, like ants. Or bees.

Every time I cry it feels like I'm doing irreparable damage to my eyes, like they're joining the heap at my knees. I'm beautiful. So was she.

Perhaps, she didn't feel it at first. Death is slow when it drowns you with honey.

06.25
the coffin

I've worn my hair differently today. Did you notice?

I figured if anyone would notice it might be you.
You're the ones who've been staring at all those
photos of her. You've got photos of her, don't you?
That's your job, isn't it? To take photos? To look at
them. You must've noticed her hair.

I never wear a braid, so it feels a bit odd. Definitely
unlike me, but I'm just following orders. I know,
they're unspoken ones, but I pick up on things, easy.
I'm good at anticipating needs. And I'm doing what's
asked of me, even if no one's asked. I don't want
anyone to have to ask me to do anything. So, I antici-
pate the need and act before the asking.

I expect the box will feel better today, now that I've
accepted it.

I don't know The Managers, but I know what's expected of me.

Plus, it's what she would've wanted.

06.25
disco girl

I can feel you wanting to know when I knew. You
think I must've been the first one to register what
was happening when she—

My box is next to hers. I told you that myself. But
after that night in the parking lot, I went out of my
way *not* to look at her, not even by accident. I was
too afraid she'd be there, staring at me again, eyes
wide and jowls sunken in, hands over her ears, slowly
crushing her skull between them.

Maybe if I had looked, I'd have seen it all happen.
Maybe I'd have seen the moment life left her lips.
Why it left so silently and lingered there in her box
for the rest of our shift, and after the lights in the
lobby went out, and after we all climbed into our
cars and she didn't follow, and we left her there, not
knowing we were letting death lie in her box over
night. Maybe I'd have something more to tell you. But

she stayed all night, a blur on my periphery, and, at some point, on that final night, I must've seen her golden form flicker out. But I couldn't tell you when or how it happened, because I refused to look.

I still refuse to look.

I know I'll see her there again, eyes wide and jowls sunken, asking me to help her.

06.26
the poet

You think I'm more observant than the rest. I might
be. I like to think I am, but I'm not special here. All of
the girls are writing inside their boxes. Maybe they
don't have the ink or paper to do it with, but I'd bet
there's one of them who's written even more than me.
Someone's filling seven hours taking detailed notes on
everything she feels without realizing she's writing
essays under her skin. I don't know what they do or
where they're from, but I reckon one's a scientist.

06.26
the naked one

You know, before last night, I thought I was making someone up.

It's the same someone I think I'm seeing over and over, even though I've convinced myself they're nothing more than a trick of the shadows and light.

I only ever *see* out of the corners of my eyes anyways, since I'm not supposed to look. But, we get bored, you know? And our eyes are drawn to people, you know? This person, though, is so tall and long and not quite filled out. Less of a person than something in the shape of one. If I didn't know any better, I'd think it were a couple of wisp-thin kids stacked in a trench coat who'd snuck in to see the girls in their boxes on a dare from their pock-faced friends. But I do know better, because I've seen it now, up close.

The other night was a special one for me. I always

get people ogling—no difficulty in guessing why—but this was, as I said, special, because the one that lingered on me last night was the person-less person. That big, dark shape slipping through the crowd, like oil. I almost hadn't noticed it this time, slinking around, before it stopped on me and stayed looming in front of my box. Despite what it might sound like, I am actually good at my job, so I didn't look into its face, as much as my bones were begging me to. I was really so good, because it stood there for ten, twenty minutes, an hour. It was absolutely violating. I'm not for that kind of looking at, you know? But I didn't look back, or send a sneer its way—yes, I say *it* because part of me can't believe that *it* is really human. I behaved myself. I asked myself, *Are these the eyes I feel, burning me all the time?* I knew the answer was *no* as soon as the question entered my head. I'd argue there weren't a pair of eyes inside that head at all. No head at all. Just black smoke.

Then, just as I was getting too comfortable, it held up a finger and tapped on the glass. Like I was a turtle. And I think that it sounded too dense for a finger. Less like skin, than bone.

06.26
the one on the bed

They found her with her fingers twisted into her
face, with her mouth and eyes wide open, locked in a
silent scream.

Or with dozens of papier-mâché bees in her stomach.

Or lying peacefully with her eyes closed and thought
she was sleeping, so they didn't think to wake her.

Wasn't she bleeding? From her eyes or tongue or
something? Hadn't she gouged out her own eyes?
Hadn't she bitten off her tongue?

Didn't she suffocate and leave little powdery marks
from where her fists were hitting the glass?

She drowned in honey, is what I heard. They didn't
know until they cut open her lungs and it came

oozing out onto the table. Someone had to taste it to be sure, is what I heard.

There was a real bee that got in with the fake ones and she went into anaphylactic shock.

She had asthma and no one could hear her wheezing and asking for an inhaler.

She overdosed on pills before she went into the box that night, was dead halfway through her shift and no one noticed.

She slammed her head against the glass over and over until her skull bashed in.

Someone filled her box with poisonous gas, and she was breathing it in for hours and didn't know it was killing her.

She peeled the skin off her feet and got a bacterial infection and died from a panic attack.

Those are just a few I've heard. Is that what happened?

06.26
apocalypse

I'd quit if the money were bad. I'd quit. But I'd do
nothing if I could, and that's the truth of it. I have
no passion for anything. No desire to do anything of
any importance. I want to do nothing and be nothing.
Eternally.

No painting, no singing, no dancing, no feeling—really,
no wanting, most of all.

I do nothing now. I just sit in the box. It's basically my
dream come true. What more is there, outside of it?

But I'd quit, if I could. All of it.

06.26
X

I can't tell if you missed me yesterday, or if I missed
you. Either way, I had nothing much to say.

I can't see anything from my box. The fogged-up glass
works both ways. It's the loneliest one, by far, not that
you asked. Just hands on glass. Empty. Anonymous.

It's odd to see one of the girls outside of work. They
seem like fixtures of this place.

But, I saw her, a month or so before it happened, at a
party in Silver Lake. We didn't talk. I doubt she even
recognized me. That's the beauty of my box. A walk
to my car is all they get and no one's being overly
friendly at that time of night anyway. At this point,
you'd think at least one of the girls might recognize
me by the palms of my hands, but, no luck.

I didn't even know which box she belonged to, just

that I'd seen her leaving work. And then again, at the party. She was fidgety, kept itching at her neck, looking over her shoulder. Could've been drugs or could've been that she was weird. I watched her for a little bit. I can do that. It's a talent of mine. I'm incredibly talented, extremely translucent, even in day-to-day life. That box was built for me. But the truth is, even if they didn't fog the glass, no one would see me. Which is a shame because I'm bolder than all of them combined.

The truth is, if I weren't so imperceptible, I'm quite certain I would take the attention of any room I sat in.

06.26
cosmonaut

There are some things I couldn't tell you. Because you'd never believe me. But will you tell me if anyone mentions the thing that taps the glass, and what its eyes look like?

06.26
graffiti

I went to the hospital yesterday. I wasn't hurt or sick.
Just ended up there, standing in front of the big glass
automatic doors opening, closing, opening—each time,
I shifted a shoulder or foot.

What do you call a memory before it's happened to
you? It was that.

06.27
the one on the bed

Something is wrong with my box.

It's not the box, so much, as the books inside it. Someone's been in there switching out the pages. They're the same books as before, on the outside anyways. Same cover, same thickness, but some-one's come in and started changing the words on the pages. I know I said I don't really read them, just stare at the text, but that's just enough to notice something's changed.

It was just a few words at first, something slightly off about the pages. But it's not just one or two words now, it's whole sentences. Describing me. What I'm doing. I memorized this one, just to tell you about it. It goes:

She's sitting and lying and reading and straining her neck with her chin in her hands.

So, there's another fly on the wall.

Sometimes, I see The Poet watching me. I'm not convinced it isn't her. She seems the type to spoon words down my throat and force me to digest them.

06.27
eve

Tell me I'm paranoid. Maybe I'm paranoid, but I'm starting to grow nervous about the faces in the lobby looking in.

In my mind, they're always the same, because I can only think up so many faces. Everyone's a mix of the same three chins, four eyebrows, two noses. I'm not the most creative person, you know? I'm not the poet. And I'm not supposed to look at the guests, so there's no real way of knowing if they are different each time.

And that's the reason that I worry. I worry that they're not.

I think I know what my mind is capable of. And I don't think it's capable of coming up with an idea like that all on its own. I worry that it isn't my mind coming up with it at all and the real reason we're not allowed to look at the guests is because we'd see just that—the same faces each night, same chins, noses, eyebrows, just dressed up in different hats and wigs. I worry that if my mind couldn't come up with that on its own, then it might know something it shouldn't. Like it's picking up on things, on the peripheries, that I can't focus in on.

These are the kinds of things I worry about. Not knowing my own mind, or not knowing what it already knows.

I have this idea, and tell me if I'm paranoid, but I have this idea that the only reason the guests exist at all is so we can feel looked at. Is it egotistical to think that way? To feel like the rest of the world exists to perceive you. Doesn't it?

Something I see on my peripheries is a tall thing in

black, and I don't know if it's a man or an idea trying
to slip in through the corners of my eyes.

06.27
the poet

Have you met The Managers? I have. They're very genuine people. Icelandic people. They stress the importance of making an artistic statement. I appreciate that.

I realized, in coming here, that being a woman is an artistic statement in and of itself. But that much is obvious, or should be by now. Everything we say or don't say, the clothes we wear, what we choose to paint on our skin, the volume and pitch of our voices, where we place our consonants, hold our shoulders, how high the shoes we wear, how short the hemline, whether we wear underwear or not, too easy or asking too much? Whatever it is, we will be looked at. And it will determine our worth. Like hanging in an auction house.

But that's not the metaphor we're making here either.

The statement we're making here is lost on people. No one understands what it is we're really doing, not even the other girls. But the patrons aren't poets. Odds are, your average guest who comes in, stands, and looks, will be determining our worth. He'll watch and he'll calculate, adding points for roundness of breast, subtracting for hips too square, multiplying by two for those big blue eyes that refuse his gaze.

He'll be so focused on assigning worth that he neglects to notice his own reflection in the glass. That's the exhibit.

It's the people looking in, with hungry eyes, and the fearful ones standing beside them, who've come to realize they're inches away from a carnivore.

I'm lucky enough to witness it. I'm the only surveyor of the kind of art we're making here. Because I'm the only one allowed to look. And it's thrilling.

I'm starting to think it's lost on The Managers too and that they don't even know what they've built here. I wonder if The Managers built this place at all. Or if it's always been here, and they were just the first to put down money for metaphor.

06.27
disco girl

This'll sound silly but I might be developing a sensitivity to light. Don't tell The Managers. My box is all light and shiny things. But last night—

I don't know if it's always been that bright or if my eyes have changed. I'll get them checked. When I've got the insurance.

But last night was the first time I could feel the light was different. Did it hurt? Almost? But only because it was unexpected. Only because something had changed. Something I'd already adjusted to. Maybe the bulbs got changed? Surely, I'd be able to tell if someone else had been in my box though. I'd notice if someone else's breath had been inside there, I think. Just like I'd know if the bulbs were shining brighter than usual.

There's no sound inside my box, never has been. But

last night, I swear I could hear the electricity in the bulbs. Buzzing. It was the sound, in the end, that got to me. Took everything I had not to gouge out my eardrums and rip out my hair.

I'll get my ears checked too. When I've got the insurance.

06.27
the naked one

I stayed a little longer last night, after the rest of the
girls left and the lights started going out. I wanted to
see if the feeling faded when the room emptied out,
or if anyone was left lingering like I was, keeping me
in their sights.

But I found myself sitting alone, for an hour or so,
in the dark. I'd counted them each, as they'd crawled
down from their boxes, left, all of them accounted
for, and I convinced myself the feeling left with them.
With a pair of eyes blinking out the back door. But
the longer I sat, the longer the peach fuzz on my
neck stood electric. Behind me, to the side, to the
front, from below me and above. It was all around
me now, growing more and more concentrated in the
dark, every angle of me *seen*.

And now, I'll tell you something, and I know you
won't believe me, but I'll still say it because I knew

something then so strongly, so undoubtedly, no look on your face can convince me otherwise.

It's the box, with its eyes on me. All its front and back and ceiling and floor and both sides, watching. I climbed out, when the lights went down, and stood with the cold tile on my feet, just to test it, and I could feel its gaze behind me then, following. I don't know how they did it.

06.27
apocalypse

There's a group of people, I only ever see the backs
of their heads, who stand in front of her box and look
in. Just stare in. Like they're watching a show.

Have you heard of dark tourism? Something like
that. It's those people who go looking for remnants
of a tragedy. Going to Lizzie Borden's house and
taking pictures on the couch, or lying on the floor
of her stepmother's room? Stuff like that. Really
messed up stuff.

It's not in the papers yet, though, which means they
must have heard a rumor. Maybe one of the girls told
some friends and they told their friends and now
it's some sort of fringe show to come in and see the
beekeeper's box? Just sitting there, dark.

Why is it just sitting dark? Why isn't there crime
scene tape around it? You'd know. You'd be the ones

to put it there. Why are people allowed to peek inside, with their mouths agape, sucking it down their gullets? Digesting her?

Do you think they're making pins for their jackets? Spinning podcasts, or writing books about it?

06.27
the poet

I lied to you earlier.

I've never met The Managers.

And I've never met someone from Iceland.

06.28
paper snowflakes

I can tell when bad things are about to happen sometimes. I don't think I'm psychic or anything, I just
think it's an intuition.

Or maybe it has something to do with time not really
being linear and everything having already happened
or happening all at once? I think I can feel it
happening, all at once, sometimes. And mostly in the
box, when I sit and I feel time moving. But time isn't
moving, is it? No, it's really standing still. Just as
we're talking, right now, having this conversation, I'm
dying somewhere, at an age I don't know yet, because
I'm a three-dimensional being and I can't feel time for
what it really is.

I saw a dead girl walking to her car and knew what
was going to happen to her, somewhere inside
that part of me that's already lived my entire life a
thousand times through. But, no matter what, I

couldn't have stopped it, because I'm a three-dimensional being.

She was already dead the last time I saw her, climbing down from her box, leaving out the back door, chugging a coffee in the parking lot, arriving, leaving, arriving, leaving, swatting at bees. She was dead. But I couldn't tell for certain yet. The craziest part is—the part I can't stop thinking about—is if everything is happening all at once, she's being born right now too, a thousand times over. And so am I. Breathing, dying, breathing, dying, arriving and leaving.

I told you the other day, I can feel death on me. I can feel it all over me. Like a second skin. Because, right now, in this very same moment, I'm already rotting in the ground somewhere and the world is rotting and melting and everything on the planet is drowning or choking on smoke then icing over and the continents are breaking into smaller continents and the fish are jumping out of the sea and yeast are coming to life on top of hydrothermal vents in the middle of the Atlantic and reptiles and plants are becoming giants and cells are splitting and converging together and I can feel life on me too.

Life and death exist together on my skin. And me being a three-dimensional creature is the only reason I can feel them.

But there is something bad. That's what I came to say. There is something bad that's going to happen.

Have you ever seen the tall thing in black, that waltzes around here at night? It towers over the people in the lobby, doesn't keep to the corners, keeps to the crowd, watching, waiting. I saw it the night that the beekeeper died in her box.

Or was it the night before that? Or after? Or ever? Or never at all?

06.28
the one on the bed

I brought back another for you.

This one said:

She waits for the bad thing coming. She sits and lies
and thumbs the pages and strains her neck with her
chin in her hand and grows sick of the smell of paper
and glue. She starts to grow bored, but can't sleep
with so many eyes on her, so she lies down looking out
at nothing and feels time pass. She turns back to the
text, when she's bored enough, but hates nonfiction so
much, she convinces herself she isn't made of it.

It's all true.

This really is good evidence for something. I just wish
you'd tell me what.

The apples are even worse than before, if you can believe that. I certainly can't. But I have to, because it's happening. And believe me, this really hasn't happened in all the years I've been here. Not with the changing of seasons. In the box, it's always autumn, so the apples grow the same. Did we decide that last time? That that's where the apples come from?

Has it been years?

But last night's was hard to swallow. The skin was too hard against my teeth and it hurt my gums each time I bit down. Seven hours to suffer through, because I have to eat the apple. I can't *pretend* to do it. That would break the practice and my body would lose count of the chews, and I'd just keep chewing and chewing—

I admit that I've been dwelling. I've started to think

a bit about the beekeeper? Do you think she did something that caused what happened to her? She's responsible for her own chewing, after all, if she was eating the bees. Eat enough bees, and eventually you'll get stung in the throat. Things don't just happen to people, do they? Wouldn't she have had to bring it on herself?

I've only ever done what I'm asked to. So why shouldn't things stay the same?

Do you think poison is bitter? I always thought it'd be sweet. But I guess it depends on the poison. If it is poison, then someone is trying to poison me. Maybe I'll bring an apple next time for you to try. I'll save the last bite for you, so you can tell me if I'm paranoid and if the apple's really bitter, or if this is just some new idea that's spread from my brain to my tongue.

06.28
the one on the bed

I wanted to come back and ask if it's the poet coming up with those words. Did she ask you not to tell? If I ask, I know she won't tell me. Why would she? But, you. She talks to you, just like the rest of us do. So, did she ask you not to tell?

It can be our secret. I don't usually keep those, but everyone else seems to, and maybe becoming like everyone else is an important part of my evolution. I could keep a secret too, if you give me the chance to.

06.29
apocalypse

You shitheads. If you knew about this and didn't tell us, you're dead.

06.29
graffiti

I about dropped dead when I saw her. Scared me half
to death. I still feel it in my face, the fear. Jesus, it
scared me. I don't remember ever being that scared.
Remember what I said about being afraid of her ghost
turning up? Well, this one's it. She looks just like her.
Just like her. Golden hair long enough to sit on. They
should've told us they'd hired a new girl.

Jesus, my heart. I could hear my heart in my ears that
entire shift. They should've told us.

I thought to myself, *I'm about to live the rest of my
life not being believed about this.* About seeing a
ghost. But it wasn't her. It's not her ghost. I keep
having to remind myself when I look across the lobby,
It's not her ghost. But I tell you, I really thought I
was going to throw up. Throwing up in the box is a
big fear of mine. 'Cause the smell would get trapped
in there. I'm really not trying to be funny. I'm being

serious. I don't want it to happen.

I started thinking about being trapped inside my box with my own vomit and then I started thinking about that new girl being trapped inside her box with the other one's ghost. And I decided hers is worse to think about. Way worse. I wonder if she knows yet. She has to. If she didn't last night, one of the girls has surely told her by now. Someone must've offered her a cigarette just so they could stand there in the parking lot and tell her whose box she's been sitting inside of, and the kind of things that might've happened in there.

I wonder how much they're paying her. I wonder if it's more than they're paying us. I wonder if she does know what happened and just doesn't care? I'd be afraid. I am afraid. I'm terrified to be around her.

She isn't right for the box, either, you know? I wonder if she's realized that yet. I don't know if the last one ever realized it. Surely, she did, somewhere near the end. Maybe taking her last breath, it clicked and she said, "Oh, I'm not right for this one, am I?"

The girl before her, though, was perfect. But that's because it was built for her. Putting new girls in old boxes always goes horribly. But no one's ever died from it before now, have they?

If there were another graffiti girl after me, I'd kill her just to spare her the shame.

06.29
coffin

I need some time to think, to let it set in. I thought
I was doing a good job. I thought I'd mastered how
to sit with one leg over the other, chin resting on
my knee, hair knit down my back, looking straight
out with empty eyes. I even thought I'd started to
hear the buzzing. I know she heard the buzzing and I
know it drove her mad and I only know that because I
couldn't hear it until I felt myself becoming her.

If you know The Managers, tell them I can be
different. I can be better. I can. I'll even lie down.
I'll lie down with my eyes closed and I'll cross my
arms over top my chest and I'll stop breathing. My
ribs won't move, my nostrils will be still, you won't
even see life moving in and out of them. I'll lay down,
become so pale, and close my eyes and hold my
breath and then I'll really become her. I can do that. I
will do that. Make sure they know. Make sure you tell
them. Don't tell them I already thought I was doing a

good job. I'll do a better one. Don't tell them I already thought I was enough. I can be more.

06.29
disco girl

It felt like the grim reaper, not a ghost. The other
girls thought it was a ghost. Truth is, I've still felt
the beekeeper's eyes on me, night after night, boring
into the left side of my face now that her box is dark.
I've felt it every night since they pulled her out of
there. Begging me to look. To just turn and look and
find exactly what I know there is—nothing.

But, last night? The rest of her came back. Except it
wasn't her, was it? They hired another girl. Not as
wispy. Not as flighty. But everything else, the same.
Same hair, same skin, still not right for that box. That
part, it feels like they did on purpose. I sure liked the
girl they built it for. She never stared, never haunted
me. This new one doesn't either. She just looks
straight ahead, focused on something, probably the
contract she signed.

But I can still feel that old pair of eyes boring into

my cheek. I wonder if the new one knows the old one's in there with her.

06.29
cosmonaut

Have you noticed that her bottom lip bleeds? All
the time. There's a little hole from one of her front
teeth, and she's always sucking at it. I try not to
contribute to rumors, but I'm just saying what I see.
Observations. I'm not supposed to be observing at
all, am I? Or am I? Would you prefer if I did? Or
didn't? Are things different now because you're here?
Contractually, though, I mean, have certain rules
been put on hold?

Will you tell them what I tell you? Isn't it your job to
know what I've seen? So, shouldn't I see it in order to
tell you? Aren't you doing this so that you can help
someone? Who? Me?

My observation is that the new beekeeper is a
nervous person, but the old one was too. Either she
was nervous all the time, or her eyes were too big
and buggy for her skull. I know the box wasn't made

for her, but she had an air about her that was well suited for it. Insect-like. Insect-air. I know her, as much as I can. Отродясь такого не было, и вот опять.

Hey. Do you know that the universe is collapsing in on itself?

It's getting smaller and darker. Everything's in a vacuum.

My box is becoming the real thing. I have my suspicions it's alive. That they all might be. I have a lot of suspicions. I have my suspicions that the universe inside my box is just condensing at a faster rate than the universe outside it. I also suspect I might be the one causing it to happen. I think the moment you become aware of the universe, it becomes aware of you inside it. And it's suffocating, really, to be known.

I was thinking today about this and wanted to tell you, because I thought you might find it funny, and thought, also, why not tell you, seeing as we're friends.

The funny thing was this: I wouldn't eat apples, as a girl, because I read something once about them having cyanide in their seeds. Of course, it isn't enough to kill you, technically, but some apples have seeds that are more potent than others. It depends on how ripe or unripe they are, so you have to be careful. I've always been careful.

I think about a time when people were still figuring out which fruits you could and couldn't eat, which ones are sweet, and which rind is most bitter, and which ones kill you. Explorers would feed new fruits to their animals, their horses, mostly, to test whether certain foods were poisonous or not. But apples? Horses can eat plenty of apple seeds and the cyanide doesn't get to them because they're such big animals. That would call for a lot of poison. A person's a big enough animal too, sure, but, knowing people, I reckon there was one who once fed an apple to his horse, and when he saw it didn't keel over and foam at the mouth, spent the next week lying under a tree eating apples all the way through and died in his own foam come Sunday. There's some sort of lesson in that, but I don't know what it is yet.

I've never asked for more than what I have. I've always had everything I need. And I've never been fond of change. I like having a practice. What I'd like, more than anything, is for things to just go back to the way they were. For me, at least. And for things to be sweet again, and not so filled with poison. Or at least in a way that stays hidden behind sweet flesh, and not in a way I can tell.

06.29
graffiti

For the record, I don't really believe in ghosts.
I don't think it's healthy to. I know you probably think I should have silly opinions on things,
because, well, look at me—but I'd rather be consid-
ered a woman of science.

I hoped to be one, once. Do you think that's silly?
That I am? Isn't it funny that I care so much?

Have you ever said a single word? Or do you wait
until I leave the room to laugh?

It's just a group hallucination, you know. That tall
thing in black. Just a contagion. People are the ones to
blame for everything. Not shadows lurking in corners.

Sometimes, I'm very sad you don't see me as a
serious person.

06.29
paper snowflakes

At first, I found it funny, didn't you? That the lobby's always empty when we first climb in and empty when we all climb out? Is this not a hotel?

I've never seen its front, never had a reason to. I've only ever come in through the back, like the others. I've heard that it's tall, with two dozen floors, three hundred windows, and painted in rouge and gold. Somebody told me that. It might have been me. I can feel its height, sitting over us sometimes. And it's easy, you know, to feel the weight of something when someone's told you it's there? So, I really do believe it.

But I've never seen the front, so I've never seen what it calls itself. It's very possible it doesn't say "Hotel" out front at all. Maybe it says "Theater." Or "Warning! Asbestos and Mold!"

It's better, I think, not to know. Imagine my own disappointment to find that they've painted it beige and not gold.

06.29
the naked one

It's sort of like taking a bath in a tub where someone
bled out.

I tried talking to her after our shift last night. Tried
to catch her on her way out the back door. But she
won't look at us, not even by accident. I can't believe
how much she looks like her. The managers have
really outdone themselves. They couldn't be sisters,
could they? This couldn't be some misguided way of
feeling close to someone that's been lost? I made it
all up in my head that they might be, because it's the
only way I feel like I could understand a reason for
her being here. Except to haunt us. The girls aren't
looking so good these days.

At the very least, I thought they'd build a different
display. Or that they'd take the last one down
altogether. Or someone would come in and bash in
the glass with a baseball bat and it'd all get swept

away into a pan with her toe prints still on the shards and we'd all gather 'round and hold hands and tell everyone our names and share cigarettes indoors and send her spirit soaring up out of the chimney singing "Kumbaya."

But, this is what happens?

This one won't say a word. She won't share a cigarette or say thanks or no thanks. But what gets me the most is how much she looks like she wants to. I worry that the honey in that box has already worked its way down her throat.

06.29
the one on the bed

I thought your job was investigation. So, tell me
why there are three hundred pages written about
me reading them? Every time I scratch my nose, I
read about it. Has the poet told you what she's been
writing lately? Has she told you it's all about me?

I don't mean to be pushy, I'm just impatient. No, I'm
not impatient. Impatient isn't a good word for it. No.
I'm *tired*. Energy is an exhausting thing to give when
it isn't returned. And I'm feeling sorry now I was ever
excited about you being here. You're not worth it and
I've turned against you. I could do what you're doing,
and I might. And I'll do it better.

You won't be hearing from me anymore. It isn't my
job to talk to you. I'll just come here, to my box each
night, and skip this room entirely.

06.30
the poet

You think she never left at all? You think she just
changed her nose a bit and climbed right back into
the box? A very elaborate prank? Maybe I'm not the
only performance artist here, is all.

06.30
paper snowflakes

Something bad is going to happen again. It's
happening right now. It's already happened. It's
happened, hasn't, then happened again, and every
time the timeline repeats itself as the universe sways
back and forth, blinks in and out of existence.

It's cold in the box. It's gotten much colder than it
was several days, or weeks, or was it years ago? I
don't believe there's any difference, seeing how days
and weeks and years are all the same amount of time,
which is no time at all. All I know, as a three-dimensional creature, is that it's colder now, a few degrees
colder each time I climb into the box.

I used to be in pain a lot. As a girl. My body would
cramp up and I'd be rolling around the floor in pain
every month. The only thing that helped was climbing
into the fridge. Shoving myself in between the milk
and rotisserie chicken, folding my torso in half,

jamming my knees into my chin to fit, while my mother shrieked somewhere in the house. Because she knew I was dead. I was dead when I crawled in and dead when I crawled out again, over and over. In some different version of now, I died in the fridge, and my mother shrieked, and it killed instead of saved me.

But, in this version, the fridge is good. Being really, really cold is good, because it gives me some other feeling than the pain to think about. It never takes it away, just gives me something else to think about.

I don't know how they knew, but the box was built for me.

06.30
the one on the bed

I apologize for yesterday. I was getting impatient.

06.30
cosmonaut

I think I've seen them a few times. The Managers. We
all wonder what they look like, but I think I know.
I think I've seen them. Tall, good-looking group. Of
course, I can't be sure. But I've convinced myself
it's them. Swedes, maybe? Aren't all the people in
Sweden tall and thin and good-looking? Or Norway?
What do you call someone from Norway? Norse?
Norwegian. That's the one.

It has to be them. Or The Managers have hired a
group of tall, thin, good-looking Norwegians to fly in
every six or so months and pretend to be them. Just
to keep us from breaking contract. It's either diabol-
ical or very wise. I haven't decided which side I'm on
yet, or if there is one.

07.01
apocalypse

I have visions sometimes of the end of the world.
When I was a little girl, I'd see them when I'd go
too long without sleeping. I never liked to close my
eyes, didn't like the idea of being in a world I wasn't
awake for.

But when I did, I'd see holes opening up to swallow
buildings and giant dragons rising out of the sea. I
knew my box was coming for me long before I'd ever
been inside it, because I was always some sort of
omen. I was a harbinger, and it was written in every
dot of flesh across my skin.

It isn't a bad thing coming. It's just the end.

07.02
cosmonaut

Hey. Do you know what happens if you take your helmet off in space? Complete brain death in three minutes. I looked that up before I took on the role. At first, I was mad they wouldn't let me show my face. I thought it had something to do with my nose. I have a fine body, I know, but—there are certain aspects I've always wished were different.

There's no oxygen in space. All of it would evaporate out of your body in half a second or be sucked out of your lungs. You'd feel it boiling out of you, fizzing out, like a soda.

The universe is so vast, but there's no room to breathe, no matter how big or small your nose is. Isn't that funny?

07.02
disco girl

Could we turn off that light?

Is it a new bulb? Or one that's going out? Some bulbs
burn brighter just before they go out. Anyways, I'm
sensitive to it. And it's different from last time. I can
tell because I didn't notice last time how bright it
was. Besides, can you hear it buzzing? Light bulbs
buzz sometimes too, before they go out, to warn you.

There's a bulb out back, right outside the back door.
It sits above where the girls go to smoke and it's been
buzzing too. Louder each time I get off a shift and I
worry sometimes about it popping and getting glass in
my hair. I've started running out the back door as fast
as I can to lessen the risk of that happening.

And then I sit in my car and the display feels a bit
brighter too. But I think my eyes just need to adjust
to the dark. But then, so does the skin on my

shoulders. I can feel it burning. Am I the first person in existence that's ever happened to?

07.02
X

I couldn't see my reflection before.

The box was fogged up on all sides, like breath on the glass, and I preferred it that way. No seeing out or seeing in. But they've changed it. The Managers, or the girls, or who else? Who else might have changed it?

It isn't the outside that's changed, but the inside.

That's just me now, everywhere I look. I'd really rather not have to be aware of myself. I liked the way things were before. When I could just put my hands and my breath on the glass and not have to watch myself doing something I used to think was simple. Nothing's simple when you become aware of what it is you're doing, not even breathing.

I feel like I'm being punished.

07.02
coffin

I'll lie down with my eyes closed and I'll cross my
arms over top my chest and I'll stop breathing. My
ribs won't move, my nostrils still, no life. I'll lie down
and close my eyes and hold my breath and then I'll
really become her. I can do that. I will do that. Make
sure they know. Make sure you tell them. Don't tell
them I already thought I was doing a good job. I'll do
a better one. Don't tell them I already thought I was
enough. I can be *more* than enough. She isn't her. I
am. She isn't her.

You never told us how she went out.

You're really doing me an unfairness.

How can I really be her, if I don't know how to lie? I
don't know if I should lie with my skull bashed in or
with bees in my stomach. Are my cheeks swollen or
hollow or pimpled with red welts or flecked with

blood? Knowing would change the way I become her. I just want to do a good job. I don't believe I have yet. Because I know they've sent the new one here for me and only for me, and that they'll do away with her once I've proven she's no longer needed.

I'm being sent a message and I don't like the sound of it, but I'm also not the type to plug my ears.

07.03
paper snowflakes

They'll say her box wasn't built for her. That it was made for the one who came before. Right? You've heard them saying that? But can I let you in on a secret? It isn't a real secret, just something I've thought of that I don't want other people hearing.

There was a girl before the girl before, and one before her too. No one's box was made just for them, that's just a trick of the box. I was laughing and laughing after last time, after telling you my box was made just for me. I almost believed it that time. It's so easy to believe in things like that. But the truth is, the secret that I've thought up is this: no one's box was made just for them, we were all just made to fit in boxes.

It's better to believe things are the other way around, isn't it? Don't tell the other girls. I worry it might hurt them.

07.03
cosmonaut

I've started to get this nagging thought that there's no air inside the box.

I realize I've never checked. I've never been inside it with my helmet off, so what if all the air I breathe is coming in through the helmet, filtered in through the bag on my back, just enough for eight hours, and none is in the box at all? A warning to be careful with air, to not to want more than I've been given.

Перед смертью не надышишься.

I've started to worry what could happen if I take my helmet off. But it's not just the box getting smaller, it's the helmet too. I can feel it tightening around my neck. Now, it's pertinent I stress I haven't gotten bigger. I'd know if I have, and I haven't. It's the helmet and the box working in tandem. Shrinking in. My universe is collapsing in on itself. There's a black hole here somewhere and it's sucking us all in. I'm just the only one that feels it.

07.04
the beekeeper

I insisted on speaking to you, and only to you. You're
an outsider. I am too.

And I know something's going on that no one's
telling me. I know it for a fact because of what
I found.

Someone scratched it into the floor of my box. I don't
know how old it is, and you really can't see it unless
the light hits it just right, and it's hard because the
color of the light in there is so dizzying. But if the
honey light hits it just right, you can read the thin
little lines someone scratched into the glass by my
feet. It's a warning.

You could come see it yourself, if you wanted to. You
could follow me over to see it, or no. No, you could
also just believe me when I tell you. You could believe
me, even though I could be making it all up.

People never believe the things I say to them, and I think it's because my hair's so long.

It was one of the girls before me, I think, who put it there. I've taken to tracing the grooves in the glass with my finger, to keep myself busy. My fingers have taken to hiding it from the guests, or the girls, or even from me when the light hits it just right.

It's five words. The letters etched thin, like ghosts.

"You've caught it now too."

07.04
the one on the bed

It's not the same bed. I know that now. The text proves it.

It's changed, over and over again, I'm certain. I used to doubt, but now I'm certain. When I first started, it was stuffed with cotton, then foam, then straw, and now, I think, gravel.

Even at home, my bed feels harder, and I never get any sleep. I just see text behind my eyes when I close them. They're still there now. Here.

She lays in bed another night, shrugging the covers off and turning to the streetlight leaking in through the blinds of her window. It's a brighter light than before, harder bed than before. She can feel that now, with her eyes wide and mind awake. She can feel the sharp weight of each tick on the dull green radio clock beside her head, blessed with the curse of consciousness.

07.04
disco girl

Last night, the new beekeeper turned and looked at me just as the old one did. I swear, their eyes moved in sync, two ghosts caught in the same jar. And I could feel two pairs of eyes burning in unison against the side of my face.

They might be teaming up. The dead and the live one. Someone should do something about that, be proactive about that, I just don't know how or what.

I don't know what goes on in there. I don't know what sort of box it is. The type that brings dead girls back to life? I don't know what'll happen if they catch wind of each other. Last night might have been a coincidence, but how long until they start to choreograph every turn of their heads and unblink of their eyes?

Someone should help the new one. It just can't be me.

07.04
cosmonaut

Hey. Do you know what happens when there's a
shortage of oxygen to the brain? Complete brain
death in less than ten minutes. I didn't know that
before I took on the role. If the brain dies, it doesn't
mean *you* die. It means you'd have to be on a venti-
lator for the rest of your life, a long plastic tube
down your throat, keeping you alive. But that doesn't
sound much like being alive to me. That sounds like
being held hostage.

I'd rather it happen in space. I'd rather burst into a
million pieces and fall into the sun.

I know what happened to the beekeeper. I saw the
whole thing, just didn't realize what I was looking at.

I think I'm becoming too aware of the universe and all
the things that happen inside it. I'm not quite sure

how to make the universe unaware of me, but I
suppose I could take my helmet off.

07.05
X

I play this game sometimes called *am I pretty or am I young*. Now that I'm walled in with my own reflection. I never know how to win it.

What am I and is it beautiful is a different game entirely. And it's not for the faint of heart.

But it passes the time.

Isn't that all we're doing here?

I used to try so hard to be friends with other girls. It got harder as I got older to sit around a table with them. It's not the fact that they're women, it's the fact that I should be more capable than I am of feeling my own womanhood. It should be innate, shouldn't it? The undeniability of me being a woman? I am one. I feel it in every part of me. I feel it in the hot weight of my cheeks, in the salt in my eyes and corners of my mouth, in the color red. But I was never so undoubtedly a woman that it ever became part of my identity, and I think that's the issue. I could never sit at a table full of women, filled up with all the same symptoms as them, and have any idea how to make it clear what I am and have them believe me. You don't know how hard it is to want so desperately to be something you already are. Or maybe you do. Maybe that's really what kills us.

07.05
the beekeeper

It isn't there anymore.

They've gone and buffed it out.

My finger is bored.

I shouldn't have told you anything. I was wrong.

07.05
disco girl

It's just too bright, isn't it? You've made the bulb brighter somehow than last time.

Are you the one I should be afraid of?

You've gone and made it all burn brighter than before. I know why. I know why. I know why. I know why. I know why. I know why.

07.05
cosmonaut

Пока мы не встретимся снова.

[no recordings were taken the day of 07.06]

07.07
X

It's a little historical, is what it is. We've never been given the night off before. No one answers your emails, so you just come in regardless of what you need. We didn't know until we showed up today. And we're already here, now, anyhow, so I might as well talk to you about it.

It'll be weird to go a night outside the box.

All I heard was the screaming. You can't imagine all the places my brain went. Not as many as hers, maybe, bad joke to make, but—I hardly even heard the thuds. I thought someone had come in with a gun or that there was a fire or something. *At any second, I might be yanked out of this box by my hair*, I thought.

But it was sort of peaceful not knowing if what was happening out there could even get to me. The only thing real, when I'm inside the box, is the box and, well—me.

I was the last to know what she did.

07.07
apocalypse

There were guests there last night who saw it happen.

That's the only reason we're not in today. Someone's too afraid of not being able to sweep it under a rug like the last one.

Hey, I—

I think we all might be sick with something.

07.07
the naked one

I don't think I can talk about it yet.

I heard the sounds before I saw anything. It was a breach of my contract to even look. I never realized that might be in the contract to protect me from what I might see.

07.07
graffiti

She'd been weird lately, hadn't she? That's what people always say isn't it? She was unhappy. Different lately. I couldn't put my finger on what it was. Maybe her body. Maybe the skin on her face. Maybe her hair. Girls change their hair especially when something's the matter. Didn't she change her hair? Or was that someone else? Are we allowed to do that? Is that in the contract? Didn't you write the contract? Wouldn't you know? Who are you, again— what—what are you doing here?

Anyway, she did it herself. I know because I watched her do it. I'm not saying that doesn't make it less sad. It is sad, it is, but—guess they'll have to change her box now. To something more fitting? Humpty Dumpty, perhaps?

That time I *was* making a joke. And I see now that it wasn't a very good one. You know what? Forget I said anything at all.

It's just sad. I want that to be left on the record, and none of that other stuff.

07.07
eve

Did anyone mention the sound? I was surprised how loud it was. Well, the part where she cracked. Perhaps that's why they'd always kept her in a helmet.

I fear I'll never feel the way I used to again.

07.07
paper snowflakes

Didn't I know this already?

Didn't I say I saw it? I knew it. It's okay. I'll tell the girls it's already happened and hasn't happened yet, all at the same time. It'll help them to know that, so they won't have to worry when it happens again. I'll let them know we're three-dimensional creatures and these things happen and people split their heads open one moment, and are clean and whole the next.

Yes. Because that's how things happen in theater.

07.07
the poet

Between thuds, I heard the laughs.

There's a moment when people don't realize the
reality of what's actually happening and they laugh.
It's like their brains short circuit to keep them from
feeling what comes next.

I don't blame them, because they didn't know what
they were seeing. It was performance art. Until it
wasn't. Right?

I might have laughed too. I might've thought, *now
this is ridiculously theatrical. Now this is Broadway.
No, a haunted house. Unrealistically extreme.* But
then, *bam*, and boy, what a metaphor. All of the
sudden, a metaphor, not even Broadway could show
us. The universe is so vast. The universe is nothing
compared to the one inside our heads. We've seen
that now. Brain splattered across glass like a network

of stars.

As a girl, I watched a woman on the train who'd lost her face somewhere in the midst of imagining what it was a woman should look like. She had some version of one on, big bulging lips and alien cheeks, that had been built up on top of her own, and then built up again and snipped and shaped until she no longer looked like she'd ever known her mother. I kept spying over at her, peeking between the pink carpet seats, as she spent the whole three hours of our ride setting timers and lying back as she pressed strips to her nose and eyelashes and cheeks. I don't even know what she was doing, what it was for, just that it all seemed very unreal. Very Broadway. Very some-form-of-art I couldn't understand. And I thought it was funny, until it wasn't, and I laughed, until I didn't, and I realized I was seeing a person who was sick with something.

But boy, what a metaphor.

I'm not sure I like the kind of art we're making here.

I'm not sure this is at all what I set out for it to be.

07.07
coffin

What's happened?

Well, I've split in two.

07.08
paper snowflakes

Is she really at a hospital, with a ribbon around her head, keeping her pieces all bound together like a bouquet? Or did someone start that to make us feel better?

You know, I used to have this dream as a kid, have I told you this before? I don't remember who I've told this to and who I haven't. It just seems like something I might've told you. Stop me if I have.

I used to have this dream, as a kid—why does everybody have such trouble hearing about other people's dreams?—it was that I was walking through an aquarium on a field trip. I did go to an aquarium once, on a field trip, so that explains that.

I was walking—but really, they're not so boring—through this—other people's dreams, anyways. I'd listen if someone thought it was a good enough story to tell. It didn't happen in this realm, but that's just fiction, isn't it? Why do we like fiction when someone invents it, but not while they're sleeping?—

I was going through this aquarium, and I'd stopped to watch the penguins for a while in this big blue room. I'd knelt down in front of the glass and could smell them, like stinking horses, and I was absolutely mesmerized, but when I came to again the room had gone quiet. My class was gone and most of the other tourists had cleared out. So, I continued on to the next room and the next, stopping to watch the jelly-fish and turtles and, the whole while, the world each room over was growing dimmer and more and more blue, like the air was becoming the sea. All I can do to explain is to say I felt suffocated, or drowned. And at what I thought should be the end of the whole thing, I found myself in a long, glass tunnel. A big, long clear tube where you can watch the fish swim over your head, and you feel like a crab on the floor of the ocean? I could've stayed there for a long time too, marveling up at the world I was suddenly a part of, but up ahead, coming from somewhere, was a thudding. *Thudding*, and *thudding*, and coming from the far end of the corridor, so I headed towards it. But it was a dream, so no matter how far I walked, the tunnel stayed ahead of me, but the thumping kept growing louder, so I knew I was headed towards something. And I did get to the end of the tunnel eventually, but it wasn't a door to the cafeteria or light spilling out from the gift shop, it was another wall of glass with the whole ocean behind it. Miles and miles of impossible water.

And behind that was the thing thudding against the eternal wall of glass. The only thing between me and the ocean. A hammerhead shark, bashing its head up against the tank.

I stopped being able to move then. I could only stand in place and feel the thuds knocking at my knees, pounding against my ribs each time his big flat head met the glass. I just stood there, dumb, and watched as little hairline cracks started webbing out across it and little pink wisps of blood slipped into the water. My legs begged to turn and run, but my eyes stayed hungry, knowing what would happen when the shark thudded its last thud, but needing to see the moment the skin broke away from its skull.

Then, there was a cracking, like thunder before lightning strikes the ground and I thought it was the head breaking open but it was just the glass with the whole ocean behind it.

I should've put a hand up to stop it.

Didn't I tell you about my dreams already?

07.08
the naked one

I was posing so well the whole time. It's kept cold so my nipples stay sharp, and I'm perfectly round where needed, and my skin is even all over, and I look absolutely edible, but do you know who they were watching once the show started up?

I was right about that, wasn't I?

07.08
the one on the bed

I didn't know what to do with myself, really. The other night, I mean. I found myself painting my toes. It felt like the calmer thing to do. Paint my toes. I laid on my bed. My at-home bed, not the one here. That much should be obvious seeing how we weren't here at all, which is why I didn't know what to do with myself.

It's in my body now, I guess. I guess I'm sick with it now. My right knee aches to curl up to my chin and my arms long to lay, like a monkey's, prodding at the soles. It felt like the right thing to do then, to sit at the window, with me looking down and out and them looking up and in.

And all that time I never picked up a single book. Like I said before, I'm not much of a reader.

07.08
coffin

I saw her eyes flicker up at me, evil, just before she bore her skull in.

You're next, is what she was trying to tell me. Trying to, anyways. *You're next*. Perhaps because I've been doing my job too furiously and too passionately and others can't stand when that catches people's attention. She thinks I had it too easy, with the way the other one left us, and took it as an opportunity to give me more difficult work. She was hoping I'd have to partake now, afterwards, day in and day out, with my face on the glass. With my skull smashing on glass.

Her only mistake was not seeing it through.

I have the coffin after all, not the hospital bed.

07.08
the beekeeper

What's that tall thing in black that stares into my box all night?

07.08
eve

I know that it went on for three whole minutes. I know that because somewhere in me is counting by chews and swallows.

She's ruined it for me. Every bite feels like the crunch of her skull between my teeth. The flesh is just flesh against bone, and it spills out wet and acrid since I've started biting her in two. And I think I'm being poisoned, but it isn't happening in the way I assumed.

The brain tastes bitter, is the thing. It's the original sin, isn't it? The brain, and being born with it? How lucky to be born without one and be God's favorite child. I've eaten up so much brain by now, I might be sick with something. With the sin, perhaps, her sin, all filled up with it, all bitter. I can't be to blame. But her, I'd like to.

07.08
the poet

Boy, what a metaphor,

to think a woman might be more,

than a metaphor for something.

I used to be a poet.

I won't write anymore, now that the rules have
changed. Now that you've tricked me into being a part
of some statement I'm not sure I understand. If I'm
not a poet, then I must be some other *thing* in all of
this. If there's one thing I won't do, it's lack meaning.

07.09
disco girl

I have to put on sunglasses each time that I talk to
you because you're trying to burn me up with all
this light.

07.09
apocalypse

Things here are going to absolute shit, by the way, so you know.

You know what I realized? I'd never seen her face before. I'd only ever seen her inside the helmet. So, I didn't know, not only *what*, but *who* I was seeing, when it started. I thought maybe it was a guest, or someone who'd crawled inside the box when no one was looking, someone off the street, someone more suitable, in my opinion, for losing their mind.

But you know what else I realized? What else is really bad news? I realized she'd never been anything but her box, to me. A fixture. What a shame it is to be a fixture, really. For any of us, really. I guess that's what we all are. Our boxes. But we're not the ones who built them. Did we? Did I do that? And I'm beginning to think my design was purposeful, but not kind.

I really think we're sick with something.

07.09
the beekeeper

I can't stay here. I know that. I can't leave either. I know that now too.

07.09
X

Why do I wish I'd seen it? I hate that I didn't get
to see it. I keep imagining what it looked like in my
head. What is that?

I had a fear of going blind as a child. I used to cry at
sunsets, and arched doorways, and different depths
of water, scared of the day I'd wake up and not be
able to see them. I was in love with shape and light
and texture. The way light bled through leaves to
hold the dirt in its fingers. How whispers of quartz
cut through rocks on the side of the road while I
walked, picking up on the glitter that concrete side-
walks fill your eyes with. I looked at everything as
deep as I could and as long as I could stand, certain
one of those times would be the last. I looked at
everything aside from myself, of course. Because
where's the glitter in that?

I knew what the box was long before the other girls

started catching wind of what we'd signed up for. Mine always felt like the most direct attack, even before I could see myself in the glass.

I know everyone goes through life thinking they're special, until they accept that they won't be. I tried accepting that too, but it always felt like I was betraying something. I know what I am. I know there's some prevalence in me, good or bad. It could be that I'm evil. Do you think it was Satan's persistence, that he too could be as illustrious as God, that sent him down to Hell?

Either way now, I remain unseen, except by myself. I'm all I can see. Before, though, I didn't realize that was an advantage. Nothing here is a complete trap. They always give you a way out. It is not the end of my life. It is not the end of mine. It is not.

07.09
the naked one

I did see more than I thought. I don't like to stare too long at the picture of her I keep in my head, but I have to think about terrible things, or else I'll fall asleep at night too easily and become well rested.

I'd always noticed the colors of the girls in all their soft pinks and browns and whites. I hadn't memorized the shades of her particular face, given that it always stayed hidden beneath her helmet. But I did look, once I heard the thudding, and I noticed her nose, like a warrior's, like Athena's, archaic, something to paint.

With a nose so bold, most wouldn't pay any mind to the color of her lips, but I noticed them in the seconds between each time her skull hit the glass. I couldn't miss a color like that, amongst a room of pinks and browns and whites. And I wondered if lips are always blue in outer space, or if that's why she was trying to get back down to earth.

07.09
[unlabeled]

everything here is perfectly designed

transformed from one degree of glory to another

but still i wonder if ending the world would be a good
or bad thing

07.10
graffiti

I went to the hospital yesterday. It wasn't the one she was in, but I forget there's more than one in the city. I'm not even from a small town, but hospitals, and where they sit on a map, aren't something I think about.

I went looking for her, though, at a hospital, I suppose. I really just peregrinated—wandered—into one and surprised myself. I was driving and didn't know where to, and ended up in the visitor parking lot and didn't have to convince myself to go inside because my legs were already on their way. It felt kind of like going to the grocery store. I'd amble the aisles and find her, with her face in two distinct parts, tied together with ribbon.

But listen. Really, actually listen.

Do you ever come to and feel your body and realize

you've been walking around in so much silence? It's like getting out of a movie you've gone to see by yourself. There's all this sound and music and you're somewhere else for a while, outside your body for a while, and then when you leave and the night's so quiet, it starts to crush you?

And then you realize the world has been incognizant—unaware—of you as long as you've been silent, and you're just moving through it really, cutting through it, like a knife? Don't laugh. Days will go by where I don't talk to anyone. I've realized that. There will be five, six days in a row, where if I don't call my mother, I don't make much sound. And I begin to cut through reality like a knife wherever I walk. In the cereal aisle, like a knife. Nodding at the cashier, like a knife. Moving through the floors of a hospital without moving my lips or popping my knuckles, like a knife. Like a surgeon. Like a surgeon scientist.

The world could blink and I'd be gone, and the only thing it would be lacking is my breath.

I found myself wandering beige halls, peering into even beiger rooms, hoping I'd find our cosmonaut, whoever she is, with her head wrapped up in ribbon, and I'd open my mouth and the knife would clatter to the floor and I'd be a celebrated part of the earth again.

Then, I realized, I don't remember what she looks like. And I'm not sure I've ever really looked at anybody, especially myself.

What do you call that feeling when you've been somewhere before but don't know when or why? It was that.

07.10
the beekeeper

I know what happened to the one before me, and I
have my own ideas on how it did. It's in my contract
not to speak with the other girls, but that doesn't
mean I don't listen to them or watch them. I've
come up with the idea that it was all of them acting
together. Like an Agatha Christie novel or something.
Things from books can happen in real life, you know.
Not everything always stays made up. In this story,
there are girls and there are managers, but they're
one in the same. And everyone here is in on it but me.

You know, I've looked in the papers and it isn't there.
It should be written down somewhere and it isn't.
How can it be that a whole roomful knows what
happened here to the one before me, yet it's nowhere
to be found?

I know you aren't the police.

07.10
coffin

My dream might be to be King Tut. I was never sure what I wanted to be until now. But King Tut, the boy king, is a realistic next step. To lie like a royal, with my eyes closed and chest still, would be the greatest honor. I'd finally have the respect my art deserves.

I'll move into some museum. A sarcophagus made of gold. The pay won't be as good, for sure, but it's my dream. I'd never have had a dream if I hadn't had the box show me what I was made for.

And thank god I know what I want now. Thank god to this place for showing me. What is it? Isn't there some saying about that? How does it go? Some meta-phor, maybe?

07.10
the poet

It's my duty to protect them, now. I feel that in my
bones. I'm the watcher, the one who sees. I'm less
like a god than The Managers, more of an archangel
than the others, they're just humans. I'm on a cloud.
From here on out, my box will be "heaven" and my
name will be "Michael," and I will hand out blessings
instead of poems and I will still not be a fortune
teller, but I will be able to dream up some sort of
future for us. And while we're here, we'll be isolated
on our own earth, now that we no longer have our
extraterrestrial. And we're a planet populated by
women who live in hives, and women who paint their
toenails green, and women who eat apples poisoned
by God and claimed by the devil.

My first blessing is this: may we remain untouched,
unchanged, and endowed with the clarity given by six
glass walls. May we all be duchesses of our realms

and do our jobs, and nothing but our jobs, and enjoy
the tasks we've been chosen to perform.

The world ends sometimes so it can grow life from rot.

07.10
disco girl

I'll be the next, I suppose. To go blind and fall
through the glass.

You're so tall. I never noticed before, but you're
so tall. And what color is your hair? What color
would you call that? I'm sorry. I never cared much. I
thought a long time ago these talks with you might
have ended, but they've gone on and I never doubted
it was right to keep them going. I almost look forward
to them. To you. You're my greatest friend. I've
known you all my life. You're like a sheet of glass and
look just like me, if I picture us both inside out.

You don't listen to me, though, when I'm talking,
because it's still so bright in here, so you couldn't
really love me, which means my heart is broken.

07.10
eve

Don't tell the other girls this—well, I suppose you'd get in trouble for that. Would you get in trouble for that? Does this work like a doctor's office? Are you allowed to tell anyone what I say in here?

Well, I think I might be leaving. I sent an email to the managers. They've never written me back before, but I thought maybe given the circumstances.

Maybe *given the circumstances.*

I don't know if this is one of those situations where you just leave and hope the box hasn't gotten big enough to fit what looks like the rest of the world inside it. I hope this isn't one of those situations where you leave, and every time you look out a window you see the tile floor of the lobby and nondescript faces looking up.

I can't keep chewing and chewing.

07.11
paper snowflakes

You know, I used to have this dream as a kid, have I told you this before? I don't remember who I've told this to and who I haven't. It just seems like something I might've told you. Stop me, if I have.

I used to have this dream, as a kid, that I was walking through an aquarium on a field trip. I did go to an aquarium once, on a field trip, so that explains that.

I was walking through this—I was going through this aquarium and I'd stopped to watch the penguins for a while in this big blue room. I'd knelt down in front of the glass and could smell them, like stinking horses, and I—

07.11
apocalypse

.

What do you think's catching around here?

Has anyone complained of a strange heat? Like we're
in the belly of something?

I learned something once about fire. It only exists
on earth, because it's made of carbon, and so are we.
You can't start a fire without a living thing, or a thing
that was once living. We're all the fuel in the earth.
We can't survive without ourselves, without things
that are living, without things that can catch. You
have to burn one thing to give life to another. We
all know the sun can't provide enough heat to keep
things from freezing over. So, we have to fight for life
by burning ourselves up.

Maybe we've been catching fire here. Maybe it moves
through the air like the thoughts in my head. Maybe
that's what it is.

Maybe the thoughts in our heads are leaking out from hairline cracks in our boxes and catching fire inside of everyone.

07.11
X

I worry, now, we might forget about the first girl, now that the second's in our sights. I couldn't sleep the other night because I was trying to remember the beekeeper's name, and then I realized I never learned it in the first place.

07.11
the one on the bed

Do you know how hard it is to read in the dark? It's making me blind trying. Now that they don't want me to see what's written on the pages, I'm trying even harder. First, the guests stopped coming. Then, the lights went out. They were out one night when we came in and they've been out ever since.

The only way we know how much time has passed is with our bodies. Once the little one finishes with her apple, we know it's time to leave the box.

I've been spending my time evolving my eyes to read without light. It's incredible what the body is capable of. Last night, I read:

The bed is harder. Just a slab of rock now, with a sheet tucked across it. She's becoming a scholar. If she could read faster, see better, she just might huve made it to the end of the story by now. She's scouring for fore-

shadowing, is what she's doing, wasting good time,
though, because she'd spoil the whole thing if she
could read between the lines.

07.11
Michael, The Archangel

The box is whatever I decide it is. That's the power of
my box. Same as before, isn't it? Isn't it? No distrac-
tions, just what I have to offer. The giver, not the
given. The artist. Making art!

I've been feeling unmonitored. I have white feath-
ered wings. I have nine turquoise eyes. I have
golden light beaming out of my body that burns at
an alarming rate. And it's a blessing; I'm still an
exception to the rule.

I give blessings to the girls, when they're looking
down. The giver! Blessings, not poems, not scribbled
on paper, but in the bow of my head. They're playing
mortals, all except for one; and another that keeps
rising from the dead; and another that can't wait to
join me in heaven.

The other two are not here. They must be trapped in a

world between worlds, some limbo now. Some empty place sealed in by glass on all sides, souls trapped by their indecision on whether they belong up or down.

From the clouds up here, I've begun to figure things out. I've begun to question my superior.

Do we really think it was the little one's sin that gave her cause to bite that apple? Or was it because God gave her a curious mind, and then punished her for it?

Thank you, I designed it myself.

07.12
apocalypse

We'll keep coming back, you know. You don't have to try so hard. You don't have to be kind or make us feel safe. We'll keep coming back, because, when the world ends, things here will stay the same.

There will be pockets of sameness scattered across the world, when the mountains come down. Refuges no one knows about. In some of those places, we'll just go on, without realizing what's happened outside. We won't notice the subtle changes, like the ground growing wetter, or the air growing hotter, or the fact we're eating lava in our bowls of Cheerios instead of milk.

And we'll scratch stories into our glass-bottomed caves and become feral and then civilized again and I want you to know this is a very true prediction. It was written in the stars of the box she shattered her head against in an attempt to get out of eternity.

07.12
disco girl

I don't like the lights being off. Not completely. I'm afraid of the dark.

As drastic as this all is, though, it does feel good to be listened to. I just didn't expect you to get rid of the light altogether.

It does feel good, though, to know that you really do care. That you really do love me.

07.12
eve

I won't swallow anymore. It isn't an act of rebellion, but of self-preservation. I thought the box was made for me.

Who are you anyways?

I can't keep chewing and chewing and chewing and chewing and chewing and chewing.

07.12
graffiti

There's no hospital, silly. There's no hospital. I think I've been to every hospital and they're all just hallways with the same person in every room. And no room with its head split open. I'm not sure where I heard the rumor in the first place, that she was in one. Now that I think about it, I'm not sure I heard anyone ever say that at all. Was it you? Was it you who told me? I'd have believed it, if it were coming from you. I trust in you, entirely.

Anyways, I've been to every hospital. You know, there are a lot. A lot in the whole entire world. A lot of sick and hurt and dying, and I think I'm discovering something, and I don't think it's good news.

What have you done with her body, then, if there's no hospital? Where is she suffering from?

Did you leave her in her box to lay with the blood and

glass? Did you leave her in there to turn into some-thing intrinsic—no—interesting, to look at and just decide to keep the lights off? Is she in there now? My eyes are not accustomed to the dark, but, even if they were, I wouldn't look for her inside it.

She could be in there with her eyes wide open right now saying: "There's no hospital, silly, there's no hospital. There was never any hospital, and I've bled out by now. I've soaked into the floor."

I've narrowed down all possible evidence and know now there's no hospital. I am a woman of science. I'm a serious person who believes in serious things, and I believe we are in something really very serious now. Please, don't laugh, please. Don't laugh. They're just words.

07.12
the coffin

I sat there, breathing in the dark, when it came down
upon me like some great hand pressing its warm
thumb to my skull and filling me up with realization.
I'm being contacted. The way they send messages is
different from us. The Managers don't answer questions or give instructions or commendations in the
same ways we do, but that doesn't mean they don't
send them at all.

Nothing here is random. Of course it isn't, it's all
fixed. There are no random acts of violence or unex-
plained tragedies. That stuff doesn't happen in the
real world. No, this is all set up, all of it. It's all been
fixed up, for me. I know that now. The Managers
must think I'm so stupid. It took me so long to figure
it out. The other two girls were a Morse code. They
were a dots-and-dashes way of telling me my real
purpose here. Teaching me to be Tut.

You know, I am the only one in the world who knows what it's like to be dead? I didn't realize the gift I've been given. Death is supposed to be the end of everything, but I've beaten it. I am the only one in the world who's descended into hell and been forced into resurrection in a big gold sarcophagus.

I'm the most powerful being alive because of it. I owe The Managers the life that can no longer be taken from me.

07.13
paper snowflakes

I guess, as long as I can remember, as far back as I can think, I've seen skulls bashed against glass. It's everywhere these days, you know, impossible not to come by, something so common like that. The girls keeping the shops on Rodeo, one minute they're adjusting the mannequins in the windows, next thing you know, all their broken bits are scattered across the glass, hairline cracks running up and down shop windows. All the windows out there on Rodeo Drive. Look close enough and you can see the places where a skull's fallen in.

It's so commonplace, you probably haven't noticed it. Not so much a trend as a necessity, you know? Certainly, not a pandemic. Just the only logical next step. So, what I'm saying is, I understand why she did it, the cosmonaut, because it was the logical next step for her, like so many others. Like the girls in the shops.

Ask any of the girls here, and they'll know what I'm getting at. They'll have seen it too, I'm sure of it. I'm sure any woman's found themselves at a nice place, sitting with their steak and their Malbec and they'll hear a *thunk*, *thunk*—and look over and see a hostess slamming her skull against the water cistern—*thunk*. Pouring out everywhere. Wet and pink. Sort of like her lips. Sort of like her labia.

Once I realized how commonplace it was, I stopped worrying so much about what happened with the cosmonaut that night in her box. We leave wet pink footsteps wherever we walk, and we forget that sometimes. Things can be so isolating here, and we forget that sometimes.

Like the other one, with all her bees. We were all so shocked when it happened, but in here it's so isolating, we can forget sometimes it's not so uncommon to die without good reason.

07.13
graffiti

Do you not take me seriously? You always sit there,
so unmoved. I've made a massive discovery. I've
done something incredible, but you sit unmoved. You
make me feel ridiculous. I hate you. It's worse than
laughing at me, all the not saying anything at all.

07.15
Michael, The Archangel

The little one's gone. Have you noticed?

The light in her box is on, but it's just a tree in there
now, no one to pick the apple. It is tempting though,
isn't it, sexual and red?

Eden was always a trap.

07.17
X

I know the beekeeper's name. I'm not supposed to, am
I? Will something happen to me now that I know?

Anais. Salt Lake City.

There's a big family back there she hasn't seen in
years who don't know where she went or why or
if she's here or there, or alive or dead, or a famous
ballet dancer. They don't see much ballet, so how
should they know?

I know more than they could know, and I never knew
her at all.

I know she gave up the church and came to California
and that's the last time that they spoke. I know she
lived in a studio in Koreatown and her landlady took
in her cat when she stopped coming home to feed it.
And I know she was allergic to bees. And that she

was hard of hearing.

I'm the only one in the world who knows that Anais, Salt Lake City, is dead.

Kaiya. Ontario.

07.19
the naked one

If I go silently enough, I don't think anyone would be the wiser.

I'm starting to think no one's rented a room for much longer than we might have thought. Long before they barred the doors and turned off all the lights. If no one's coming in to check on us, will they know if I'm gone? Or will the money keep coming when I've walked through the back door and forget to ever walk back through? There's a reason they leave it unlocked.

Sometimes, I wonder if all of us left this place a long time ago, long before the guests stopped coming, but we're stuck here whenever we sleep. It would explain why our emails are never read. It would explain why the door's always open.

I wonder if you're the only person here who knows we're dreaming.

07.21
apocalypse

We were never told to climb back inside our boxes,
but we did. Even after the guests stopped coming to
look at us. It took me a while to notice they'd stopped
coming in altogether, and at first I wondered where
The Managers had put them. I guess I supposed they
worked here, like us, had a set list of rules they had
to follow, night in and night out. A set list of things
they could say. Recycled wigs on their heads and
masks on their faces and contracts signed, set to
watch us and never watch each other. That, at the
end of each night, they filed into a broom closet and
closed the door to sleep before the next one.

It still feels right, even without them there to look in
at us, to spend a night inside the box. Inside a pocket
of sameness.

Didn't I tell you it would be this way? That we'd come
back when the world ended?

Don't you have ears? What are you?

07.21
the one on the bed

She's still isn't much of a reader. She isn't too keen.
Yet she reads and reads and can't help herself from
thinking the words are made of her.

They just say that now, over and over. I'll rewrite
them. I'll become an editor and I'll put it all back in
place. Erase that part about the beekeeper,
the cosmonaut.

Liars.

What is this place?

You're not the police. So, what is this place?

I figure I've figured the whole thing out. I sit before
you, oozing investigation. I am sexier now than I was
before. I'm thinking of burning the books to hide
what I know because I know that with knowledge

comes fear and I really can't be tricked into believing instilling fear is power. The writer is mistaken if they think I wouldn't go and burn myself up. But if the words are made of me, then they'll stop if there's no source for inspiration. It could be dangerous to start a fire inside a box, could be deadly.

But that's what you want, isn't it?

I'll wait. I'll sit and I'll ooze and when the timing is right, I'll go all up in smoke.

07.27
eve

I just wanted to come back one last time. To see if it was sweet.

07.29
the one on the bed

It was the naked one taking the bat to her box.
Thanks to the dark, we didn't know anything was
happening until we heard the *crash*, and the glass
came tinkling down across the tiles, sharp little teeth.

We thought she'd come and bash ours in too, and
we'd fall onto a biting pile of ourselves, but she put
down the bat when she was through and sat on the
glistening hill of what used to be hers. All skin and
freckled spots of red.

It's a real hazard here now. The room is a maze of
paths cut through fields of glass, yellow brick roads
to and from our boxes. It is nice to see a use for
the bat. I'd always wondered what its purpose was,
waiting for so long, propped up against the wall
like that.

07.29
disco girl

Am I bleeding?

I think I've got glass in my eyes.

07.30
paper snowflakes

My feet are a mess. I'm sorry. My feet, all cut up and tracking red all over the place. I'm all cut up from carving a way to my box. It's an unbelievable amount of glass. You wouldn't believe it. More than I thought one box had in it. It covers the floor. I had to wade through to get to you and now my feet are all cut up.

There's not as much as I might have led you to think there is. It's just hard to see where you're stepping when the lights are off. But you feel it. *Oops*, wrong turn, wrong place to put a foot down. But that's part of the job, I guess. And we're really very lucky to have one. Have you seen what's going on outside?

07.30
the naked one

Are you angry with me? It wouldn't matter if you
were. I wasn't acting out of reason. I wouldn't be
unreasonable. I just wanted to ensure that there was
nothing left for me to come back to.

08.03
the coffin

I nap for the longest time and it's peaceful. It's the deepest I've ever slept. I am everything while I sleep. Alive *and* dead. I'm the cycle of it all. It lives in the gush of my cells. Everything that is and ever has been is in me now.

I don't fear what's going on outside, because it's inside too. That's where it comes from.

08.05
graffiti

I came today to kill you.

I was on my way here and decided I had to do it. It
wasn't a hard decision, really, once I realized you've
never said anything at all. You've never even asked a
question, you're just here, day in and day out, sitting
with two chairs and a recorder running.

So, I stopped again at the hospital and grabbed a
scalpel off an operating table, and it all felt so
familiar, what's that called? Or maybe I stopped by
the kitchen store and bought a knife block and
emptied it out in the parking lot and picked the
sharpest one to tuck inside my coat. I don't know
what I did, but I also don't know what I did to
deserve this.

I couldn't stop thinking that if I cut you, there
wouldn't be any blood. There wouldn't be any wires

either, just empty black space beneath the skin. Has the world really ended? Are you really here just to break the news? Am I really that special?

No one comes to see us anymore and it's because they've barred the doors. The windows are boarded, but no one ever told us to stop coming in through the back. The lobby is dark, but we've been sitting in our boxes each night waiting for the lights to come on. Those are the serious facts.

So, If I kill you, two things might happen. Either the lights will come back on, or go out forever. Whichever happens, I'll quickly forget you ever existed at all.

Is this what science always comes to?

I'm not here to hurt you. I just want to kill you and

that'll be that.

08.10
disco girl

What happened in here? You're not the same one as before, are you?

Is that what you've always looked like? I don't trust my eyes. First, they filled up with light, and then dark, and now glass.

Have you seen the news? It's awful. The world is a horrible place. An unsafe place. What a choice. What a choice this is.

Hey. I've made up my mind about what happened. Now that the lights are down and there's no more buzzing in my ears, I've decided the end of the story. The whole story and my end for it. What I've decided to believe in.

In my story, there are no Managers, just the girls in their boxes. Just us, and we've brought this all on ourselves. Believe me or not, it's my story. Have you heard this version of the story yet? It's the only thing I can believe to be true right now. All these earthquakes, all these floods. It rained fire some-where yesterday, burned a whole village down, all the women and children died. Their bodies melted in the snow. It rains fire even in cold places and there's nowhere good to hide. They're dying in droves, bodies blasting up to bits. Pieces lie everywhere, hands and feet scattered across the globe, growing up out of the soil, and everyone keeps asking for help, reaching up out of the ground with their dirty nails, dirty fingers.

Might as well take what you've been given. That's the other only thing I can believe to be true right now. There's no pessimism in me. It's joyful when you understand your situation. I won't even ask for help. I'll just keep coming back, as long as the back door stays open. I have four walls I can see through, a floor, and a ceiling over my head. I'm one of the lucky ones who stopped needing to look up to someone they've never met.

I'm brighter than I've ever been.

08.22
paper snowflakes

I've decided they found a bunch of bees inside her.
It feels so good to not have to go on not knowing. To
have some sense of closure. It feels so good, deciding
what's right and what's wrong and what story I'm
part of. I would hate to leave a story unresolved. To
have them throw tomatoes.

The box is the only safe place. It's the only place
where time can't touch me. And I would like to stay
there forever. I've never cared that it wasn't made in
my image. I fit inside it comfortably.

09.01
Michael, The Archangel

The statement we're making here is lost on people.
No one understands what it is we're really doing, not
even the other girls. But I am in awe of this place in
the dark.

You're the only surveyor of the kind of art we're
making here, with empty boxes and glass on the floor,
and you with your recorder running and running
off into oblivion. Making art feels so like making
violence. You must feel like God.

So, end it.

Бьёт - значит любит.

He beats what he loves.

Отродясь такого не было, и вот опять.

This has never happened before, and yet, here it is again.

Перед смертью не надышишься.

You can't postpone death by taking a deep breath.

Пока мы не встретимся снова.

Until we meet again.